death writes
A Curious Notebook

Darlene Barry Quaife

ARSENAL PULP PRESS
Vancouver

DEATH WRITES
Copyright © 1997 by Darlene Barry Quaife

ARSENAL PULP PRESS
103-1014 Homer Street
Vancouver, B.C.
Canada V6B 2W9

The publisher gratefully acknowledges the support of the Canada Council
for the Arts for its publishing program, and the support of
the Book Publishing Industry Development Program, and the B.C. Arts Council.

Art Direction by Russ Bugera
Illustrations by Cathie Hahnel
Printed and bound in Canada by Webcom Inc.

CANADIAN CATALOGUING IN PUBLICATION DATA:

Quaife, Darlene A. (Darlene Alice), 1948-
Death writes

ISBN 1-55152-038-9

1. Death—Miscellanea. I. Title.
HQ1073.Q34 1997   306.9   C96-910481-0

To the dogs of winter.

To all those whose support I have enjoyed,
"May you escape the gallows, avoid distress, and be as
healthy as a trout."

"Clasp the alphabet to your heart, though there are tears in every letter. I sing in your little ear, let sleep come, a little handle closing a little gate."

Anne Michaels, *Fugitive Pieces*

"Familiar things happen, and mankind does not bother about them. It requires a very unusual mind to undertake the analysis of the obvious."

Alfred North Whitehead,
Science and the Modern World

I FOUND THIS BOOK in a coffeehouse. It was left on the corner table I frequent. But not in the form you now hold in your hand. What I almost discarded with the bruised and flaccid newspapers littering my table was a "scribbler," an exercise book issued to grade school students when we still had one room schools that taught penmanship and Latin as a matter of course. This scribbler is a plain, square collection of lined and unlined pages. A buff cover with a place for the student's name, name of his school and teacher. Inside is cheap paper divided into sections headed by letters of the alphabet. According to the outside, this exercise book belonged to

> Student: Elsie Cole
> School: Coleman
> Teacher: E. A. McGillicuddy
> School Division No. 1216
> Year: 1921

On the inside page I discovered in wide, black felt-tip letters, **DEATH WRITES**.

Below each letter of the alphabet is a line or two of faded handwriting most probably copied there by the original owner, Elsie Cole. It would seem that when teacher E. A. McGillicuddy issued the scribblers, s/he had the students transcribe sample words they could use to practice their penmanship.

The author of *Death Writes* has not ignored Elsie Cole's well-rounded words. This notebook is arranged according to the alphabet and responds to many of the words written 75 years ago. Death observes, thinks, and writes, and *Death Writes* is a wry, eclectic, profane and profoundly amusing meditation on life by Death. S/he is articulate, knowledgeable, irreverent, and nothing escapes his/her gimlet-eye. Between the lines of wit and wisdom, Death doodles.

After *Zz* the scribbler is free of student penmanship. Using the ubiquitous felt pen, a title page has been created for this section of the scribbler, **DEATH NOTICES**. Here Death has collected quotes, clippings and curious bits of this and that.

I refer to the author as Death, because the perspective of this notebook is Death's. This is Death's take on life. You will have to decide for yourself whether Death keeps his/her felt-tipped pens in a plastic pocket protector.

– Darlene Barry Quaife

DEATH WRITES

Art is the sex of imagination.
— George Jean Nathan

Aa

a persona a persona grata a persona nongrata a persona impropria

A dark winding street somewhere, Amsterdam perhaps, where an abattoir and art gallery are neighbours. The storefronts are indistinguishable, unremarkable, the same face presenting different bodies. I follow the health inspector into the abattoir. My mistake. He is dressed in black like an art patron. Everything is white — walls, floors, counters, doors — white file cards spin in a Rolodex, the meat is alphabetized by cut, located by locker number. Next door, the art gallery walls are stripped down to red brick, the floor covered in sawdust, blood drips from carcasses hanging in the rafters. I am issued a black umbrella at the door.

I adore silk stockings
I abhor sackcloth and ashes

Adams, Ansel
1902-84
U.S. photographer
famous for his landscapes
of the Western States

Ansel Adams photographs in every restaurant washroom throughout the west, black and white on black and white. His subjects never grow old, only grimy. Photography is a pox on Father Time, but he has decay on his side. "Subjects are subject to decomposition," this warning should appear on all photographs

Acquired a dog today, will call it Anubis

The Ancient Egyptians had guts and knew how to store them. No gloom and doom for that bunch. Embalming rooms were called "the house of vigor" (rigor mortis to vigor mortis) and black was the colour of rebirth. The pleasure of eternity depended on the dog god. Anubis took the human soul between his teeth, as gently as a retriever with a dead duck, and deposited it on a set of scales balanced by truth in the form of a feather.

ANUBIS
jackal god of
funerals
please return
to owner

Bb

bravery bat baptism bit beastiaries big Bingen batty blow

NAME THAT BEAST

MATCH	SYMBOLIC TRAITS	BEASTS
1)	diligent, unenlightened & aimless, holy creatures to the goddess of farming	APE
		CRAB
2)	wisdom, hatred, holy creatures of the sun, strength, longevity, high rank, god of dance, vanity, greed, lechery, god's spies	VULTURE
		PANTHER
3)	envy, good fortune, virtue, natural death, intelligence, fallen angel, vigilance, fertility, shrewdness, timidity	MOUSE
4)	chaos, misrule, protection from hail, hypocrisy, fertility, fortune, power, greed	DOG
5)	loyalty, guardian against ghosts, companion of necromancers, guide in the afterlife, unclean, uncontrolled wrath, marital fidelity	CROCODILE
6)	needs human urine to protect itself against poisoning, "fragrant" voice, cunning, enemy of	BAT
		ANT

the snake, savage, associated with Christ,
aggressive women, shaman

7) the soul, demonic and prophetic powers, originated
from the mud of the Nile, lasciviousness, female
sex organs

8) gift of prophecy, associated with childbirth &
motherhood, visitor to the "towers of silence",
symbolizes the Virgin Mary, longevity

9) misfortune, rain, "casting off of the old Adam,"
enemy of snakes, bravery, pregnancy,
imprisonment, baptism, rebirth, the grave

The name game! I spy with my little eye something that
is peculiar. No. No. No. Give up? People! Peculiar = People.
Proof? This odd obsession with putting a human face on
animals and insects, fish and fowl, not to mention bowls,

> "The name of a man is a numbing blow from which he never recovers."
> — Marshall McLuhan

jugs, combs, chairs. Nothing is safe, most things are sacred. So, what's with this naming thing? What drives people to label the seen and unseen, the clean and unclean, the mean and unmean... enough, enough! A humble form of homage? Sometimes. Take that bit of fur suspended between leather wings. Medieval bestiaries put this spin on the beast, "When bats decide to stay in one place for an extended period of time, they hold on to one another and form clusters — an exchange of favours of a sort quite rare in human society." So says UnterKircher according to Biedermann. More names!

Homage? Perhaps. Humble? Hardly. The measuring stick here is human society. And it's a big stick. Everything comes up against it. Name denotes value, value on the human scale. "In ancient China the bat was a symbol of good fortune, primarily because of the homonymy (sic) of the words for 'bat' and 'luck' (fu)."

> "Names are but noise and smoke,
> Obscuring heavenly light."
> — Goethe

While the ancient Chinese were painting pictures of lucky bats, others were concocting bat recipes. Waste not, want not. All creatures are pressed into human service. Some 800 years ago, the flittermouse could be found in the medicine chest of St. Hildegard of Bingen. Her cure for jaundice was batty:

1) "carefully impale the bat so that it remains alive"
2) "attach back of bat to back of patient"
3) "then remove bat and attach to patient's stomach"
4) "leave on patient's stomach until bat dies."

The sixteenth-century Flemish botanist, Clusius, came up with two hundred new names for two hundred "new" species of plants in Spain and Portugal. Didn't they exist before Clusius?

Beast Key: 1) Ant 2) Ape 3) Bat 4) Crocodile 5) Dog 6) Panther 7) Mouse 8) Vulture 9) Crab

Cc

circus carnivorous carnage charnel cannibals capitalism Columbus

Discovered Scratch & Sniff today. A page in a magazine that commanded me to perform this act. Scratch what? Sniff where? Surely not a portion of my anatomy? (Although I have observed this practice in social settings, particularly at sports events.) But no, the directions referred me to a card protruding from the taut spine of the magazine.

Impregnated! The card was impregnated with scent. I buried my nose in the slick folds and closed my eyes. The pages became the petals of a huge redolent flower, the card a stiff stamen. In my desire, I scratched so hard my fingers tore the card and underlying pages.

Up came the smell of flesh. Hot as a circus tent in summer, the sawdust steaming, giving off the smell of wet hair and boiled flaxseed. In the ring, the scat of carnivorous animals mixes the jungle with the savannah with the prairie.

Tigers to hyenas, coatimundis to coyotes.   Under this big top the acrobats dye their tights with incarnadine — the colour of flesh, raw flesh, blood red. Their legs flash carnage. There is no bone-white bone. Carnification fleshes out memory in crimson. Under the skin of a carnival tent, carnal knowledge invades fantasies. Smell the flanks of roan ponies and bareback riders, the haunches of lions and tamers, the quiver of elephants and mahouts. The death-defying feats of tightrope walkers, trapeze artists, human cannonballs electrify the ozone with the sweet odour of danger, a whiff of the charnel house meant to thrill and terrify.

I had scratched the surface of an article on carnivals. Then one on cannibals and the next on consumerism. I marvel at the schizophrenia of magazines:

I confer with Hieronymous Bosch

"The Caribs, an Amerindian race of northern South America and the West Indies, were anthropophagous (man-eating). In Cuba, Columbus heard what he thought was the word 'caniba:' the Cariban name for strong men. While the Caribans were saying 'calina' or 'galibi,' the Spanish were hearing 'canibal.' The Spanish and then the English turned strong men into cannibals."

The shape of human desire?
The dark circle of an open mouth.

"Publicity is the culture of consumer society. . . . Capitalism survives by forcing the majority, whom it exploits, to define their own interests as narrowly as possible. This was once achieved by extensive deprivation. Today in the developed countries it is being achieved by imposing a false standard of what is and what is not desirable. . . . Publicity turns consumption into a substitute for democracy." (John Berger)

→ *freedom of choice between —*

cappuccino & latte, Ford & Mercedes,

Levis & No Name, Jeep & Hummer,

paper bags & plastic bags,

Timex & Rolex, Cohibas &

just a cigar.

☺☺☺ Consume thyself

I confront Hugh Hefner in every room of his Playboy mansion.

Cirque du Soleil is reincarnation. Hieronymus Bosch and I sit in the audience and watch the Circus of the Sun performers put on the flesh of animals. In spandex skins of gecko green, chameleon caprice, lizard lemon they climb poles, hand over hand, measured, mechanical, reptilian. A French Canadian Garden of Delights.

Dd

deplore duchess dance death dervish defied distinction danger day die

The whirling dervish taught me to dance. They dance to
defy the body.

Dancing dogs at the circus! I love the human
circus, deplore the animal acts. Unnatural acts. Poodles
in pompoms, terriers in trousers — as banal as
alliteration. That's what is so appealing about the
Cirque du Soleil: humans imitating animals.

Reading The Duchess of Malfi. I'm moved by the
courage of the woman, her keen insight. Sent a copy
to Isadora, she is my greatest regret. She refuses to
speak, not just to me. She utters no sound. I'm to
believe her creativity, her voice is strangled. Isadora
Duncan expected to dictate her death, as she had
her life. I expected her to laugh outrageously at

her death, it seemed so right. After all,
what better place, what better time?
Nice on the Mediterranean, September, 1927.
That young Italian mechanic smitten,
desperate to impress a mature woman, a great artist, shows
up in a Bugatti racing car. Isadora wraps herself
in a painted shawl for the ride. He starts the car.
She flings the shawl over her shoulder, the fringe
catches in the spokes of the turning wheel. Strangled,
she dies instantly. Not so, the Duchess of Malfi.

DUCHESS.   What death?

BOSOLA.   Strangling: here are your executioners.

DUCHESS.   I forgive them:
            The apoplexy, catarrh, or cough o'th'lungs
            Would do as much as they do.

BOSOLA.   Doth not death fright you?

DUCHESS. Who would be afraid on't?
          Knowing to meet such exellent company
          In th'other world.

   Neither the Duchess nor Isadora played it safe.
They both defied convention, imposed their individual
wills on society. The Duchess insisted on her right to
choose a husband without consulting her family. A woman
of her social class in 16th century Italy was the pawn
of her male relatives. The Italy of the Borgias was
better known for its intrigues than its freedom of
spirit. She was a class act among cowards.
Her rings were not hiding places for arsenic. Greed
motivated her brothers to order her execution, but
they also wanted her to repent, to break her will.
Having none of their own, they didn't count on
her courage.

BOSOLA. Yet, methinks,
The manner of your death should much afflict you,
This cord should terrify you?

DUCHESS. Not a whit:
What would it pleasure me to have my throat cut
With diamonds? or to be smothered
With cassia? or to be shot to death with pearls?
I know death hath ten thousand several doors
For men to take their exits; and 'tis found
They go on such strange geometrical hinges,

```
                    You may open them both ways: — any way,
                        for heaven-sake,
                    So I were out of your whispering; — tell
                        my brothers
                    That I perceive death, now I am well awake,
                    Best gift is they can give, or I can take.
                    I would fain put off my last woman's fault,
                    I'd not be tedious to you.
EXECUTIONERS.  We are ready.
DUCHESS.       Dispose my breath how please you, but my body
               Bestow upon my women, will you?
EXECUTIONER.   Yes.
DUCHESS.       Pull, and pull strongly, for your able strength
               Must pull down heaven upon me: —
```

This is a story Isadora could dance. The Duchess
is as powerful as the women of Classical Greek

Tragedy. Agnes De Mille has said, "Isadora was a wild voluptuary, a true revolutionary. She flouted every tradition.... She tried to enforce a new code of human behaviour and was outspoken as few people ever have been." So, her silence is a purgatory of her own making.

Isadora, the mother of Modern Dance, and I should be partners. My Danse Macabre achieves the ideals she strove for: the elimination of social distinction, the equality of men and women.

LIFE IMITATING ART

#1: Bugatti, Italian car manufacturer, his full name was Etore Arco Isidoro. Isidore: Greek from Isidoros, "Gift of Isis, the Egyptian goddess, wife

of Osiris. Isadora, the feminine form of Isidore.
Osiris: Son of Re and husband of Isis, he
succeeded his father as King of the universe but
was murdered by his brother Seth. Restored to life
by Isis and Anubis, he became lord of the afterlife."

#2: "On September 14, 1926, she (Isadora) gave
a joint recital with Jean Cocteau and Marcel
Herrand. Isadora danced the poet's Orpheus.
Cocteau then read some of his recent poems, one
of them entitled 'Danger of Death.' A year later,
to the day, Isadora would die."

Ee

"Master of the endgame," that's what my longtime chess partner calls me. We're at our regular corner in the coffeehouse, at our regular time, the board before us, but my mind's not on the game. I'm in need of advice. A latter day colleague of Carl's, Clarissa Pinkola Estés, has invited me to the theatre, more specifically a play by that contrary Irishman: Beckett's "Endgame." When I tell Jung this, he has a right good howl. At times he can be quite undignified for a Swiss doctor. Some of this mirth stems from the knowledge that theatre is not my thing. The rest of his joy, of course, is in the title of the play. I fear there is a conspiracy among the Jungians, they conspire to have a little joke at my expense.

Now, I'm not a Philistine. I happily frequent art galleries, get quite nostalgic at museums, dance is a drug I imbibe, I have a cracking good time at the circus. But plays present me with more shades of grey than I'm capable of seeing. Basically, I'm a rank and file literalist, black and white, not that I don't enjoy a good pun, play on words, metaphor, the occasional symbol. Mind you, symbols have gotten me lost in airports and rail stations. An enigma, all those pictographs, open to interpretation, not to mention the ones that have been negated with a circle, stroked through with a line. As I recollect, the circle has always been a positive symbol: sun, moon, canopy of the heavens. Only a computer would find "no" in a circle. To the Platonists the circle is a perfect form. The Egyptians expressed eternity by tying a piece of string in a circle. The ancient Greeks had Uroborus, the snake devouring his own tail. The medieval alchemists adopted Uroborus as their "mascot" and appropriated the astronomer's sun symbol, a solid circle, to represent gold. Concentric circles, a design that can mesmerize if stared at, swirl over megalithic gravestones. Reminiscent of circles in a pond when a stone is dropped cleanly into the water, could it be that the concentric circles symbolize sinking into eternal sleep? The circle inside the square: the divine held within the symbol of the earth. The negative is nowhere to be found, not in the Zen Buddhist's

circle of enlightenment, not in Chinese
duality — the circle containing Yin and
Yang. So, Paul Arthur has a lot to
answer for.

Paul Arthur, a Canadian: Paul Arthur, a
godfather of environmental graphic design. Trust
a Canadian to come up with a prohibition sign.
The ⊘ is Paul Arthur's. He had pedestrians not
ghosts in mind at the time.

At this point, Dr. Jung accuses me of
buying time with a mouth full of words. The
endgame is afoot. King hunting has begun. But I
am more interested in the Jungian moves of Dr. Estés,
than the mating moves of Dr. Jung.

"Why has she invited me?" I ask. "Why me?
Why that play?"

"She wants your impressions. Beckett's a

visionary." Jung has not raised
his eyes from the chess board.
    "So that's it, I'm a guinea
pig. This is research. You wrote something about
visionary artists, didn't you? And she wrote that
book, <u>Women Who Run with the Wolves</u>."
    "Beckett's a paradox. You two have much
in common."
    "I should go then? That's your recommendation?"
    "Enjoy!"
    I tip over my King. "I resign."

"Use your head, can't you, use your head, you're
on earth, there's no cure for that!"
                    – Beckett, <u>Endgame</u>

Ff

THE WOMAN WHO ATE FLOWERS

She would simply appear in the garden, glance toward the house, place a flower petal in her mouth and walk on through the gate to the river. No matter the weather, she came, rising with the river mist, in the waterglass light after a rain, in broad daylight. Surprised by her presence in his garden and her singular act, once she was gone all he could remember about her was the flowers she ate. He kept a record. Gradually he began to notice the true shape of her clothing. Its simplicity made it unremarkable until he realized he was not seeing a real skirt, but the flowing legs of skirt-wide pants. And her coat was really a burnoose, made popular by such orientalists as Sir Richard Francis Burton. This confirmed his speculations that she was a visitor to his quiet part of the world. Perhaps recently returned from the East, one of those women adventurers his sister so admired.

Her presence in his garden was compelling, so much so, that he awaited her, moving his desk to the window, calling for food, tobacco, anything a servant could bring or do which meant he did not have to leave his lookout. Instead of tending to the work of fiction he was writing, he contemplated the list of flowers she ate.

Why, he needed to know, did she appear daily to feed on his blossoms?

The mysterious woman had not gone unnoticed by the man's

sister with whom he shared the house. Her rooms were on the second floor above his and her windows also looked out on the garden. His sister was keeping her own diary of flowers consumed, but was quicker to discover their meaning. In her library, she had a copy of G.W. Gessmann's guide to <u>Blumensprache</u>, the symbology of flowers.

Over the course of a week, the woman in the burnoose had put to her lips the petals of: WHITE HYACINTH (DAY ONE), WHITE ASTER (DAY TWO), BINDWEED (DAY THREE), TOBACCO FLOWER (DAY FOUR), IRIS (DAY FIVE), LILAC (DAY SIX), YARROW (DAY SEVEN).

The woman stayed away for five days and when she came next she ate: FORGET-ME-NOT (FIRST), GRAPEVINE (SECOND), WHITE LILY (THIRD), WHITE ROSE (FOURTH), THYME (FIFTH), RED ROSE (SIXTH).

The man broke the code the day his sister left. The mysterious woman never came into his garden again.

Blumensprache (1899), the language of flowers and love:

Aster (white): "Your true friendship lessens the torment of my misfortune."

Bindweed: "No gaze in the world is so keen, so deep, as the hawk's eye of love."

Forget-me-not: "Three words reveal the wish to meet again: Forget me not."

Grapevine: "Move closer and remain true to me."

Hyacinth (white): "My heart draws me to you, pale dreamer."

Iris: "You fill my heart with joyful hope, only then to plunge it into doubt."

Lilac: "In your every look and word speaks the beauty of your soul."

Lily (white): "You are as innocent as this symbol of innocence."

Rose (red): "Yes!"

Rose (white): "No!"

Thyme: "Unity of souls is the greatest good."

Tobacco Flower: "You awaken feelings that slumber sweetly within me."

Yarrow: "Are you in fact as unaware as you would seem?"

This little story I will give to Emily. She's always delighted when I'm romantic. I've also found her an old board game we can play, although I must return it to the Musée du Cinquantenaires before they miss it. Belgians can be so pernickety. There'll be the devil to pay if I have to take it back after the alarm's been raised. But I couldn't resist. Senet is Emily Dickinson, Emily Dickinson is Senet. Senet is the ancient game of fate, the game of the netherworld. It will not be wasted on Emily that the game begins at the moment of death and the players race for "everlasting life and nonexistence." There are no ancient game rules with the rectangular box, so I borrowed a set of directions from Matthew J. Costello and tucked them in the little drawer with the Senet game pieces — ten lions and ten dogs:

Most Senet boards consist of 30 squares, called 'peru,' or houses, organized into three rows of ten houses each. The journey on the board symbolized a journey to the netherworld, the desired goal of everlasting life and nonexistence. The game began at the point of death, and the object was to reach square 26, the Beautiful House (the place of mummification), with all of your pieces, then square 29, the Ship of the Sun god, before ending on square 30, the House of Revival.

I once quoted Emily to T.S. Eliot. I never forgave him for calling me a 'snickering footman.' I thought he could take a lesson in humour from Miss Dickinson, so I let him have it — "We never know we go when we are going — / We jest and shut the door — / Fate — following — behind us bolts it — / And we accost no more —." Eliot's J. Alfred Prufrock seems such a whiner with his "I have seen the eternal Footman hold my coat, and snicker."

But, of course, Emily does not agree with me about Mr. Eliot and his Prufrock. She's no cynic, her sense of humour is generous.

Gg

Acquired an ant farm today, along with a painting, a cup and a large black pot. All for mere pennies I've been to markets in the high Andes, bazaars in Tibet, the West Edmonton Mall, but the suburban garage sale, now there's marketeering. There is nothing of necessity here. The place reeks of domesticity; a shrine to permanency. "A street vendor," my friend says with disdain. She prefers the old days, the old neighbourhoods that planted their garages with their gardens in the backyard. the attached garage is an abomination in her view. The car becomes a member of the family. Grass must give way to cement or asphalt. And for her, our quest is too public, the setting stark. If this was a backyard, we would enter through the gate, walk the path between flower beds and

lawn furniture, look into the life of this family:
rows of vegetables, garden gnomes and birdbaths,
moments of shadow, the smell of shade.

Margaret is impatient with this spanking new
neighbourhood. A natural sentiment in an anthropologist.
Nevertheless, we are here, in a garage that does not
smell of dark stains and cigar smoke. According
to Margaret, what you see is what you get: neat
shelves, neat stacking boxes, neat hooks, sporting
equipment, neat racks, few tools. She longs for
the Player's tobacco tins stashed in corners, on
rafters, in wooden apple crates that serve as
cupboards. To pop those lids and shake up the
contents, panning for a bit of treasure among
the screws and bolts, nails and tacks. An
old button, a chrome D that might have spelled

Dodge or Debbie (a charm from a bracelet lost in a backseat).

I chose this garage sale, so it's my responsibility to put a good face on it. I forage. I bring her a cup — "the holy grail," I say. A black pot — "the cauldron of the necromancer." Margaret assesses my offerings with a trained eye and says, "Food is the only true quest, never mind the utensils. The Christian grail is just a cup, the Celtic cauldron just a pot, unless you're a famous Swiss doctor, so far ahead of your time, you're incapable of growing old, even in name, and then the grail symbolizes the spiritual womb. So grows the soul, accompanied by the music of the stomach. Human history is written in food."

I say, "Margaret Mead, you're full of yourself."

She hands me a glass box full of dirt. "Buy this," she commands. "It's worth every penny."

Margaret has placed in my hands an ant farm. It's all she wants me to buy. Then she makes us sit on the curb, the ant farm between us. I know I am in for it. Margaret is about to salvage the morning.

"Domesticity. It's what they're good at." She points to the ant farm. "And them." She jerks a thumb over her shoulder, incriminating the whole neighbourhood, if not the whole world in a single gesture. "Food and the power to enslave other species, that's domesticity. I'm sure you know that some ants ranch aphids for their honey dew. Ant ambrosia. According to Hans Biedermann, this wasn't lost on human society. He tells us that 'In ancient Greek myth the first inhabitants of Aegina are called <u>Myrmidons</u>, ants, because they farmed the soil with antlike patience, endurance and diligence. A Thessalian legend traces plow-farming back to the invention of the important farm implement by a nymph named <u>Myrmex</u>, ant; in this civilization ants were honoured as holy creatures.' To put a finer point on it, 'By breaking up the soil and taming herds of cattle and goats, humans collided with more microbes than they had ever met before. Until about ten thousand years ago, humankind and the superorganism (bacteria) lived together in relative peace.'"

"Don't I know it. Increased my workload, I can tell you that! Farming — the plowing up of unseen worlds. With domesticity came plagues. Farming food meant farming disease. Put an end to my leisure time. Humans got friendly with animals and bingo, the family dog brought more than fleas into the hut, he brought measles. While the cow came equipped with an udder, tuberculosis and diphtheria; the revered horse carried the burden of the common cold. Although I must say things have improved in the last little while."

"I wouldn't get used to it. If Andrew Nikiforuk is right, humankind is on a collision course with the superorganism. He says, 'The march of civilization is really the story of how changes in the human economy and health have begot abnormal situations and much disease. The Harvard biologist Lynn Margulis says bacteria can assemble and disassemble all the molecules of modern life except for a few plant hallucinogens and snake venom.'"

"Guess I won't bother buying that paint by numbers kit back in the garage. It's a big one, takes lots of time."

"Humph," Margaret says.

"Out of the eaten came something to eat. Out of the strong came something sweet," is my response.

"And what is that?" Margaret asks.

"An ancient riddle."

"And the answer?"

"That's your department," I tease.

"Did you ever think it odd, that you're so playful?"

"Odd? You're name-calling because you don't know the answer. Should I repeat the riddle?"

"No," Margaret is testy.

"A swarm of bees making honey in a dead lion."

Hh

Hell is this flesh. A costume with no zippers.
A one-off garment reeking of boredom.

— Washroom graffiti

Now this caught me with my pants down. I
had not thought about the wearing of skin, what
it must mean. Lifting myself from a position
of contemplation, I took the problem back to
my corner table by the window. After a lazy
Sunday morning in the coffeehouse, I usually
wander the streets aimlessly, poking in shops,
looking in windows. But that bit of graffiti was
like the skin of a sun-dried tomato caught
between back molars. I couldn't leave it
alone.

Out on the street, I'm looking in the
window of a motorcycle shop. Black leather jackets

on hangers are suspended from the ceiling above the motorcycles like so many disembodied riders. These jackets are second skins, basic, black, unadorned but stiff with attitude. The wearer can convert the monosyllables of flesh into a polyglottal statement. This tough piece of cowhide speaks of rebellion, adventure, romance, authority, suppression, sex. <u>Active wear.</u>

But what happens on a hot day? the second skin is a temporary measure.

A guy brushes past me. His arms are black and blue with tattoos.

Now there's a real second skin, universally available, worn by high chiefs and criminals. Four letter words lend themselves to the knuckles of human hands, done with safety pins and ballpoint pens. LOVE and HATE are handy. Since it is the custom to give with the right and take with the left, the hands on which LOVE and HATE are tattooed say much about the individual. A crude symbol system compared to the artistry developed over thousands of years of tattooing.

One of the most beautiful second skins I've seen belongs to a Scythian chieftain who lived 2000 years ago. In his time the methods of tattooing were simple, but the art was inspired. A menagerie of fantastic beasts twist up his arms over his shoulders and around to his chest. A tracery of pin pricks and soot, the creatures of imagination — winged monsters, griffins, curl-tailed cats, snakes — roam with the animals of the Siberian Steppes — horned rams, wild asses and mountain goats. Dancing up his right arm is a deer with an eagle's head and graceful antlers that could be wings. A fish swims from ankle to knee on his right leg, placid in the company of a fanged, horned monster with a feline tail and three birds on its neck. A second skin such as this is destined to outlive its owner.

In 1947 archaeologist Sergei Ivanovich Rudenko recovered the chieftain's skin from a frozen tomb in the Altai Mountains of Siberia. Among his possessions were hemp seeds, the bronze pots they were burned in, and a small felt-covered tent. The Altai chief and his horsemen would sit in the tent, the bronze pots fuming and without doubt inhale.

Had this symbol ♲ tattooed on my left hand.

Magazine quiz: WHAT'S YOUR IMAGE?

1. Are you summer, autumn, winter, spring?

2. How many mirrors do you own?

3. Do you wear T-shirts that are advertisements for designers and clothing companies?

4. Do you really enjoy smoking?

5. Are you sexually active: same sex _____, opposite sex _____, both _____, other _____.

6. Do you collect ball caps with logos? Do you wear the peak back or front?

7. Do you drink lattes despite your milk allergy?

8. Do you actually know someone with AIDS?

9. Do you have tattoos?

10. Is your backpack authentic war surplus?

11. Do you have the following body enhancements: nose job, tit job, bum tuck, thigh suction, penis extension, scrotum enlargement?

12. What rings to you wear/where: ear, nose, tongue, eyebrow, nipple, navel, penis, labium?

My image: I am winter with a tattoo.

While I was in New York, I decided to have a chat with IMAGE 2000, WORLDWIDE CONSULTANTS This is the type of company employed by the Generals of Burma to put a user-friendly face on that country's military dictatorship. The Generals of the State Law and Order Restoration Council had to hire American hot shots; they were up against Nobel Peace Prize winner Aung San Suu Kyi. The first piece of advice the image consultants gave them: change your name. Burma is now called Myanmar. Not to someone like the imprisoned writer Dr. Ma Thida who writes, "Just call us 'Seekers of true justice'/ Not 'Burman,' 'Shan,' 'Kachin' or 'Kayah.'/ Regardless of our nationality, / One shout

of 'Do Aye' / Adds up to at
least three years behind bars. /
The distribution of three lines of
poetry / make a twenty year sentence /
In this place they now call 'Myanmar.' "

Profile
AUNG SAN SUU KYI

- Burmese woman

- 50 years old

- Leader, National League for Democracy

- under house arrest from 1989-1995

- elected head of official opposition with 82% of the seats in 1990

- holds "free speech" meetings which are against the law

Profile
MA THIDA

- Burmese woman

- 29 years old

- physician, writer and member, National League for Democracy

- sentenced to 20 years in prison for distributing banned literature

- novelist and poet held in solitary confinement without access to books or writing materials

A sample of questions and answers from my
IMAGE 2000 profile questionnaire:

Gender:	Male ✓ Female ✓
Marital Status:	Married to my work
Occupation:	recycling
Education:	extensive life experience
Community Activities:	major role
Siblings:	only child
Strengths:	- decisive - honest - egalitarian
Weaknesses:	- lingering overlong in coffeehouses - curiosity - a good story well-told
Goals:	- to be better understood

IMAGE 2000 consultant's analysis of my image past, present and future (2000 the year, 2000 the fee):

Items	Past Profile	Present Profile
1) **Physical Presentation:**	too thin	anorexic
2) **Fashion:**	drab and plain	beat generation with touch of grunge
3) **Personal Style:**	sombre	supercilious
4) **First Impression:**	inspires fear not confidence	cool
5) **Career Moves:**	ferryman, dance instructor, footman, census taker, watchman	performance artist professional witness
6) **Demeanor:**	sardonic laugh	grimace
7) **Relationships:**	seducer of the young	overly friendly
8) **Attitude:**	disrespectful of age, practical joker	chill out (favourite expression)
9) **Social Order:**	anarchist	laisser-faire
10) **Belief System:**	primitive	New Age

Recommendations toward Future Profile, managing your Image to 2000:

Recommendations	Future Profile
1) Hire personal trainer	lean, mean, muscle
2) Hire fashion coordinator	tragically hip look, shave head
3) Hire acting coach	tough, innocent, sensitive
4) Hire movement coach	poised, deep, slightly brooding
5) Hire career counsellor	virtual reality technologist
6) Hire voice coach	ironic laugh
7) Hire psychoanalyst	confirm you are blameless
8) Hire sociologist	reborn green, with reduced expectations and a sense of tribe
9) Hire political scientist	advocate for the cyber neighbourhood
10) Hire Matthew Fox	in touch with the Cosmic Christ
11) Hire ghost writer	write your memoirs
12) Hire handler	do the talk show circuit

Jj

I collect jargon the way others collect stamps, ball caps, autographs, teaspoons, nail clippings, buttons — it's the small obsessions that define us. I'm a jargon magnet.

Some recent acquisitions:

DOUBLESPEAK

negative patient-care-outcome	death
therapeutic misadventure	malpractice
memorial park	cemetery
deprivation of life	killing
death situation	dying

— Richard Lederer, The Play of Words

FUNERAL INDUSTRY JARGON

Ordinary Words	Euphemisms
Ashes	Cremated remains
Autopsy	Postmortem; Necropsy
Body fluids	Purge
Bury	Inter; Inhume; Final rest
Coffin	Casket
Corpse; Body; Stiff	Remains; Mrs. Z; Loved one
Cost (casket)	Investment
Crematorium grounds	Garden of remembrance
Dead	Expired; Passed away; Deceased
Death certificate	Vital statistics form
Digging a grave	Opening a vault
Embalming	Preservative treatment; Lasting memory picture; Preparation
Family	Prospects; Clients
Funeral	Service; Ceremony; Rite; Case

Grave; Plot	Pre-need memorial estate
Graveyard	Memorial park; Cemetery; Remembrance park
Hearse	Coach; Casket coach
Job	Case; Call; Service
Keep; Hold	Maintain preservation
Makeup	Cosmetics
Morgue	Mortuary; Preparation room
Pulverize (Ashes)	Process
Oven; Retort	Cremation chamber; Vault; Cremation vault
Shroud	Slumber robe; Clothing; Suit; Dress; Garment
Showroom	Display room; Selection room
Stillborn	Baby; Infant
Tombstone	Monument; Memorial tablet
Tools	Instrument
Undertaker	Funeral director; Mortician; Bereavement Counselor

— Kenneth V. Iserson, _Death to Dust_

A KILLING SPRING

<u>Hypoxyphilia:</u> autoeroticism due to lack of oxygen
"It's a dangerous business. The people who practice it apparently find sex more interesting when they cut off their oxygen."

— Gail Bowen

"Paris may be the only modern city directly responsible for contributing a once-technical term that is now in worldwide use to the language of death and dying. From an obscure French term for 'haughty superiority' the place in a prison where officers grilled newly admitted persons came to be known as the <u>morgue</u>.

Supercilious show of authority on the part of officials may have accounted for this development. It was a natural transition to use the room where prisoners were examined to display and to examine bodies of persons who had died under questionable circumstances. By now firmly entrenched in speech, _morgue_ became the official title of a special building in Paris where bodies of suicide and accident victims were taken until release for burial."

— Webb Garrison
Strange Facts About Death

BODY BEAUTIFUL: TRADITIONAL PREPARATION RITES

Place	Method
ANCIENT GREECE	– cremation
ANCIENT INDIA (CALATIANS)	– ate their dead
SWEDEN	– unmarried woman buried with mirror
RUSSIA	– corpse carries certificate of good conduct
SCOTLAND	– bell under deceased's head

IRAN — dead washed three times in lotus water, camphor water, pure water

JORDAN — a virgin at death is dressed as a bride; a martyr at death, the blood is not washed away

JAPAN — shave part of the head, dress in white with paperhat

KOREA — wash deceased's face with perfume

CHINA — pearls, coins, special objects go in the mouth

GHANA (ASHANTI) — rum down the throat, gold dust in the ears

— Kenneth V. Iserson
  Death to Dust

Kk

Dropped into the King's Peg for a pint; asked how the pub came by its name. Got these many versions:

"Had something to do with that disease, what's it called... 'scrofula.' Nasty bit of business, that. Glands swell up... see them bulging out of a person's neck."

"What kind of word is that, 'scrofula'? Never heard of it, myself."

"Latin by the sounds of it."

"It means 'breeding sow.'"

"Pig latin!"

"What's a bleeding sow got to do with glands in the neck?"

"Breeding not bleeding."

"The swollen glands look like piglets."

"No, you're having us on."

"Don't matter. Scrofula has nothing to do with the name, King's Peg. What Harry over there's thinking of is King's evil. People used to think if the King touched you, bang, the evil causing scrofula would be gone. The King's divine right."

"Good luck! Can't see many kings wanting to put the royal mitts, left or right, on some scruffy old glands."

"So what's the story here?"

"Pig at the trough, that's the story. Old King George, the second one, the one that had to have a drink of hot chocolate brought him before he'd get out of bed. Let me tell you, any Tom, Dick or Harry could buy a ticket to watch King George eat Sunday dinner with his family. God's truth.

"Where's the fun in that, I say?
Now if it had been that murdering
bugger, Henry the Eighth, he'd have been
worth inspecting. How many wives did
he off?"

"Just two out of six."

"No, it was more than that."

"Just two, if you don't count the one in
childbirth. My wife, she's big on the Royals. Bought
her a packet of chocolate mint bars. The wrapper's
got pictures of old Henry and his six missis on
the front, history on the back."

"Mint bars! It seems only fitting. Henry
had a big appetite, by anyone's standards. Two
and a half gallons of beer with every meal."

"Had to use ropes and pulleys just to haul him
into his King-size bed, he was that fat."

"Pegged up like a piece of washing on the line."

"My guess is King's Peg has to do with burying a king's heart separate from his body. The heart's encased in silver and wrapped in purple velvet. They've got Richard's lion-heart stowed someplace."

"Speaking of hearts, did you ever hear the one about the Duke of Orléans? Remember this from reading history. Seems, when the Duke died, way back in seventeen hundred and something, the embalmers were supposed to open him up so his heart could be taken out and put in a special box. Well, they get the heart alright, but before they can lock it up in the box, the Duke's Great Dane eats most of it."

"Oh, eh, you've put me off my meat pie, with that."

As I left the pub, I noticed a sign over the door:

KING'S PEG: A DRINK MADE
OF CHAMPAGNE AND BRANDY

LI

list loved life Lord leader last let lotus language

My Yin/Yang exercise list from a course I took last week called, <u>Taking Control Getting In Touch Exploring The Masculine/Feminine Principle Microanalyzing Dreams For the New Millennium</u> We were instructed to get in touch with the deep I-self that represents the duality of our nature: the good and bad, active and passive, black and white, etc., etc. In plain language — when you're hot and when you're not:

I

    aspire to be loved for myself
    avoid Halloween parties

    cure warts
    cycle to work

demonetize all currency
define romance as necrophilia

extol iced short schizo skinny mango
    cappuccinos with wings
extirpate egos

ghost write biographies
grandstand at hotrod races

impugn original sin
italicize life

motor in open cars (with diplomats and cats)
march with the drummer

nasalize words
never forget a face

originate graffiti
outrun time

quaff nux vomica
quote great thinkers and mad men

reserve judgement
reek of the grim reefer

salute the optimist
sandbag the sanctimonious

thieve like a crow
thrill patrons of the opera

Vaseline camera lenses
vex at bad press

zodiac with Greenpeace
zero the hours

LISTS MISCELLANEOUS

William H. Bonney

These are the killed.

(By me) —
Morton, Baker, early friends of mine.
Joe Bernstein. 3 Indians.

A blacksmith when I was twelve, with a knife.
5 Indians in self defence (behind a very safe rock).
One man who bit me during a robbery.
Brady, Hindman, Beckwith, Joe Clark,
Deputy Jim Carlyle, Deputy Sheriff J.W. Bell.
And Bob Ollinger. A rabid cat
birds during practice,

These are the killed.

(By them) —
Charlie, Tom O'Folliard
Angela D's split arm,
                and Pat Garrett

sliced off my head.
Blood a necklace on me all my life.

Michael Ondaatje,
The Collected Works of Billy The Kid

It's embalming, not embombing:

"Originally, embalming meant placing balm, essentially natural sap and aromatic substances, on a corpse. Unlike embalming, <u>embalmment</u> was the old technique of removing the internal organs, soaking and packing the body cavities with chemicals, and then allowing the body to dehydrate."

When Lord Nelson died at Trafalgar, his officers preserved his body in the ship's brandy. "The British navy still uses the term <u>tapping the Admiral</u> for getting a drink of rum."

Before embalming was commonly practised in America, "If the undertaker failed to frequently drain off the water and replenish the ice, the body occasionally exploded, and often spoiled...."

"It was a common practice to tap a leaden coffin that was bulging to let out the accumulated gas. This was done by boring a hole in the coffin and igniting the jet of gas that instantly emerged. The flame lasted from ten to thirty minutes, and the workers had to be extremely careful during the procedure."

Kenneth V. Iserson, Dust to Dust

Mm

motion masculine manufacture marionette misplaced masquerade

I'm leaving one of those dinky movie theatres packed 6 to a house (a six-pack of Hollywood's best) in a suburban mall, muttering to myself, "What's Hollywood afraid of, anyway?"

I can't get this thought out of my head. So I stop at the candy counter for a Coke. Maybe a shot of caffeinated sugar will clear the images of Arnold Schwarzenegger from my brain.

I ask the grrrl behind the counter, "What is Hollywood afraid of?"

She drops a single word with a single coin into my hand.

"Sex," she says,

leaving me with a penny and my thoughts.

I loiter about the lobby trying to decide if I should fork over the big bucks for another ticket — next show, different movie. Perhaps my misgivings are misplaced. I look for a sign, an omen. Near the candy counter there are tall plastic silos filled with plastic-bright candy (a pipe organ for a clown, that lives in a sewer, that...) I hold a clear plastic bag under the chute filled with Smarties. Pulling the handle as if it were a slot machine, I wager that if I get more than ten red Smarties, I'll take a chance on another movie.

Holding the bag up so I can peer at it from all sides, I count. Before I can find ten, the ticket-taker (who looks like a bouncer) points to the candy counter, directing me to pay.

Paid up and knowing there must be more than ten red Smarties in a bag weighing as much as a

box of shotgun shells, I make
my way to the box office.

The ticket-taker briskly
tears my price of submission.
I offer him Smarties and ask, "What is Hollywood
afraid of?" "Dying," he says, declining the Smarties.
"Shoot first, ask questions later."

I stand in line outside the bank of theatres, a
jingle forming in my head: sex and dying, dying and
sex (Ronald McDonald is singing). Are they right?

Sitting in the darkened theatre is like being in
a cave. The picture flashes on the screen and I
flashback to the cave art I have seen. Animals
captured in red ochre and charcoal. The ancients
painted what they wanted, their desires not their
fears.

Nn

net nightmare nobody noiseless nourish novelty nowhere Nelson

Punki's CyberCafe is full by
9:00 a.m. Come late, you
miss your chance at a
computer: take a number, buy
a coffee, browse a zine
impatiently. After all, there's
e-mail to be read, cyberfriends
to visit, Net gossip to pick up.
Life's full.

I'm reading the
BUSINESS & SCIENCE
section of a real
newspaper. Headline —

'Soul-catcher' computer chip implanted behind the eye

Scientists offer 'the end of death'

The Daily Telegraph
LONDON

A computer chip implanted behind the eye that could record a person's every lifetime thought and sensation is to be developed by British scientists. "This is the end of death," Dr. Chris Winter, of British Telecom's artificial life team, said Wednesday.

He predicted that within three decades it would be possible to relive other people's lives by playing back their experiences on a computer.

"By combining this information with a record of the person's genes, we could recreate a person physically, emotionally and spiritually."

Winter's team of eight scientists at BT's Martlesham Heath laboratories near Ipswich calls the chip "the Soul Catcher."

He admitted there were profound ethical considerations, but emphasized that BT was embarking on this line of research to enable it to remain at the forefront of communications technology.

Business as usual. What will they charge to live someone else's life?

The next article in the paper is about profits being made by Phone Sex businesses. I point this out to Punki, who's taking a coffeebreak at the next table. He goes to his personal, private, Punki-only computer and within minutes invites me to read the following.

TELEDILDONICS AND BEYOND

There was a young man named Kleene,
who invented a fucking machine.
Concave or convex, it fit either sex,
and was exceedingly easy to clean.

TRADITIONAL
This version attributed
to John von Neumann

The word "dildonics" was coined in 1974 by that zany computer visionary Teodor Nelson (inventor of

hypertext and designer of the world's oldest unfin-
ished software project, appropriately named
"Xanadu" ™), to describe a machine (patent #3, 875,
932) invented by a San Francisco hardware hacker by
the name of How Wachspress, a device capable of
converting sound into tactile sensations. The eroto-
genic effect depends upon where you, the consumer,
decide to interface your anatomy with the tactile
stimulator. VR (Virtual Reality) raises the possibility of
a far more sophisticated technology.

These scientific frontiers provide the jumping-
off point for the VR sex fantasy: Put together a highly
refined version of "smart skin" with enough comput-
ing power, cleverly designed software, some kind of
effector system, and a high-speed telecommunication
network, and you have a teledildonics system. The

tool I am suggesting is much more than a fancy vibra-
tor, but I suggest we keep the archaic name. A more
sober formal description of the technology would be
"interactive tactile telepresence."

"It's old news," Punki says. "From Howard
Rheingold's book _Virtual Reality_. Like he
published it way back in 1991."

"Really," I say. "What do
you think, Punki? Could I make
a business out of cyberspace
burials?"

"Cool idea."

Oo

observation oblation obitus offertory oversee oration omniscient

Upon leaving the position of chief obituary writer for a major newspaper, I decided to throw myself a wake. I put out a call for pithy quotes that could be used to toast my departure:

"After all, what is death? Just nature's way of telling us to slow down."
      —Dame Edna quotes Dick Sharples of
            Yorkshire Television

"Death has got something to be said for it:
There's no need to get out of bed for it;
Wherever you may be,
They bring it to you, free."
      —Timothy Findley quoting Kingsley Amis

"Make room for others, as others have done for you."
— Roch Carrier quoting Montaigne

"Human life is fragile, easily snuffed out by a turn of the thermostat."
— John Gray quoting John Gray

"Eternity is a terrible thought. I mean, where's it going to end?"
— Doug Coupland quoting Tom Stoppard

"Good health to your enemies' enemies."
— Catherine Ford quoting an Irish toast

"I'm not afraid to die. I just don't want to be there when it happens."
— Arthur Black quoting Woody Allen

"Life and death/ Is cat and dog in this double bed of a world."

— Carol Shields quoting Christopher Fry

"Life does not cease to be funny when people die any more than it ceases to be serious when people laugh."

— John Murrell quoting George Bernard Shaw

"When I'm dead in my grave and all my bones are rotten/ This little book will tell my name when I am quite forgotten."

— Peter Gzowski quoting the inside cover of a grade school notebook

"Two men were once out digging turf and lay down to take their midday nap. A mouse ran out of the mouth of one of them, and when it came back, the other held his hand over his fellow's mouth. The mouse could not get in again, and with that the man died."

— Robert Bateman quoting a Scandinavian tale

"Who comes?
Is it the hound of death approaching?
Away!
Or I will harness you to my team."

— Archie Beaulieu quoting Northern wisdom

"In my medicine cabinet/The winter fly/Dies of old age."

— Leonard Cohen quoting Jack Kerouac

Pp

Puck, pooka, puki, pwcca, by any name a filthy little spirit overrun with ear wax and ear hair, breath foul enough to torment Beelzebub. Puck has taken to riding airplanes. At first I thought it was just plain good luck that when I checked in at the airport for my flight to Europe, I was upgraded to first class. But, no, it was Puck plucking the keys of the computer so that I would be comfortable enough to sleep on this long journey and perchance to dream. Knowing sleep is the brother of death, Puck made himself to home in a nasal passage, my nasal passage, anchored like a mountain climber to the sparsely treed face of some mountain. I mistook the smell of him, his obstruction to my breathing, as an effect of recycled cabin air. No amount of sneezing or blowing would clear my head. Eight time zones later we arrived in Zurich.

BAR-HOTEL
RÖSSLI
RÖSSLIGASSE 7 8001 ZÜRICH

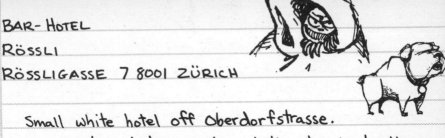

Small white hotel off Oberdorfstrasse.
3 a.m. the bar below spills out the drunks loudly
into the street. The night hot, the stone window
sill startles my skin cool as I lean out over
the noise. I sneeze and from below hear cursing
and see Puck sitting on one man's shoulder.
Lighted windows reconfigure the dark building
opposite. Tenants shout into the night. The
bulldog, night watch in the art gallery across
the street, barks fog onto the thick glass doors.
I drape my nakedness in the window curtain.

PENSIONE ACCADEMIA
VILLA MARAVEGE
D.D. 1058 - 30123 VENEZIA

Between night and morning light, stars icy cool
in a soft sky. Day heat is long gone. Grapevines
hold themselves against the arbour. The Pensione
is quiet. I open and close the iron gate as noiseless
as metal can be. The water in the canal reproaches
my shadow as intruder on its calm. I mount the
arched bridge and descend as a couple approach
out of the dark twisting calle that leads to the
vaporetto, the public boat. Dressed in evening black,
starched white, satin and lace, they are young. Coming
home before dawn from the wedding I saw when a
bedecked gondola floated a bride to the door of
a church on the Grand Canal. I pass the couple.
Her perfume makes me sneeze and Puck is

under her feet tripping up the high heels of her
party shoes. Falling toward the water, her companion
catches her in his arms. They giggle.

DUBECH
LE CAFÉ DES BONNES ADRESSES
GRAND OPERA
75 PARIS

Midmorning, Café Dubech, Depuis 1902, is homey.
The waitresses gossip and work, the proprietress and
her husband dispute the till, the pastry truck arrives.
Blocking traffic off Rue de Clichy, the delivery man
unloads a bank of trays taller than himself and wheels
sugar and spice across the sidewalk. The manager
and another woman have been cutting up towels to make

wash rags. One holds the towel taut, the other strikes it with a razor blade, wary of her staff's fingers. Cotton fibres fly into the air. I sneeze. A trap door in the Dubech floor opens, Puck sits on the edge beckoning to the pastry trays. The delivery man is stopped at the door by patrons leaving the café. The black hole in the floor slowly reveals a tall white hat, a head, shoulders, body in kitchen whites. The lift stops level with the floor and the pastry cart.

MUSEUM FÜR MODERNE KUNST
FRANKFURT AM MAIN
FRANKFURT

MMK, Museum for Modern Art. From the outside a standard box, inside a gracious building of curves, a clean building of stainless steel, a solid building of glass. Like being inside a perfect, white ear, if you look only at the architecture, not the exhibits. The walls are hung with pain — photos of street kids, drugs, violence, self-mutilation, sadistic sex, bondage. The second floor sculpture gallery: a home for the homeless. There is a real bicycle loaded with plastic bags, an old suitcase, a plastic pail — a mobile home. In a nearby room the wax torso of a man extrudes from a wall feet first wearing sneakers, socks, underwear. Waxy white legs above the socks, some black hair and sink drains set into the calves, thighs and buttocks. There's nothing to sneeze at here.

Qq

quaint quip quote quixotic quiver quick quarrel qualm

Quaint? Rarely. This list of quotes may quip, may quarrel, may seem queer sliding toward the quixotic, all meant to make quick the mind, quiver the body, cause a qualm or calm one:

"A mind too proud to unbend over the small ridiculosa of life is as painful as a library with no trash in it."
- Christopher Morley, <u>Inward Ho!</u>

"Most creatures have a vague belief that a very precarious hazard, a kind of transparent membrane, divides death from love."

- Laurie R. King
<u>The Beekeeper's Apprentice</u>

"We live in a world of things, and our only connection with them is that we know how to manipulate or consume them."
— Erich Fromm, _The Sane Society_

"Only the death of love gives more passion to the poet than does the love of death."
— Robert Kroetsch, _Prairie Fire_

"May God give you luck and put a good man in your way, and if he is not good, may the wedding whiskey be drunk at his wake."
— Old Irish Blessing

"Pellagra: Deficiency disease characterized by cracking of the skin and often ending in insanity."
— _The Oxford Dictionary of Current English_

"There is health in table talk and nursery play. We must wear old shoes and have aunts and cousins."
— Emerson, _Journals_

"One has to be able to count if only so that at fifty one doesn't marry a girl of twenty."
— Maxim Gorky, _The Zykovs_

"Good luck to you, your blood is worth bottling and may glass splinters blind hell's stokers."
— Old Irish Toast

"If, by mistake, you put on an article of clothing inside out, you were likely to get a present. To change it back would cancel your good fortune."
— John C. Chadwick,
Folklore and Witchcraft in Dorset and Wiltshire

"I decided about 15 years ago that I could not wear a tie because to me it represented, in a crazy sort of way, the colonization of my body. It was a throwback to the days of lynching — of hanging by the neck — and in the agony of my imagination I took action. I became a tie quitter."

— Molefi Kete Asante
Afrocentric Culture Critic

"The ephemeral is an essential bridge to the immortal."
— Sir Peter Ustinov
Raconteur

Rr

O thou! whatever title suits thee,
Auld Hornie, Satan, Nick, or Clootie.
                              - Robert Burns

ARABIAN	Eblis (Al Koran).
	Jinns, rebellious spirits created before man
	Sheytâns, devils.
CHALDEAN	Maskim, seven spirits which rebelled in heav
DUTCH	Duyvel, a fallen angel.
EGYPTIAN	Typhon.
	Set, the personification of evil.
	Apophis, serpent of evil.
ENGLISH	Pug, a fiend.
	Familiar spirit.
	Old Nick.
	Bogie.

GERMAN	Mephistopheles.
HINDU	Devas, bad spirits.
ICELANDIC	Puki, an evil spirit.
IRISH	Pooka, an evil spirit.
JAPANESE	O Yama, prince of demons.
	Amma, god of hell.
NORSE	Nikke, a water demon.
PERSIAN	Ahriman, darkness.
	Asuras, bad spirits.
	Dev, demon (old Persian).
	Deev, fiend (modern Persian).
RUSSIAN	Tchort, the Black One.
SYRIAC	Beelzebub.
	Béherit.
	Baal.
	Bel.
	Bélus.
	Dagon.

Dragon.

Astaroth.

Astarté

Moloch.

Militta.

Asmodeus.

Salmanasar.

Semiramis

WELCH   Pwcca, an evil spirit.

The Syriac Christians used many of the names of the pagan gods among the epithets they applied to devils.

In many mythologies the Devil is likened to an animal. The Santons of Japan call him a <u>fox</u>; the Irish, a <u>black cat</u>. Dante associates him with swine, dogs, and dragons; and in Cazotte's <u>Diable Amoureux</u> he is likened to a camel.

— David Meltzer, <u>Death: An Anthology of Ancient Texts, Songs, Prayers and Stories</u>

Ss

The beginning of wisdom is to call things by their right name.
> — Darold A. Treffert

SAINT, n. A dead sinner revised and edited.

SANITY, n. A state of mind which immediately precedes and follows murder
> — Ambrose Bierce, <u>The Enlarged Devil's Dictionary</u>

SAT, A system of standardized American college entry exams designed to nurture and reward functional illiteracy.

Originally used only inside North America, the Scholastic Aptitude Tests and their equivalents are spreading around the world in response to a corporatist desire for global fixed standards in specialized education. Consisting mainly of multiple choice and fill-in-the blanks questions, the SATs are the archetypal product of a society which believes above all in the possession of facts and the rule of expertise. In spite of "substantial revisions" in 1944, the underlying premise of these tests is that to each question there is a single correct answer.

— John Ralston Saul, *The Doubter's Companion*

SAVANT SYNDROME is an exceedingly rare condition in which persons with serious mental handicaps, either from mental retardation, Early Infant Autism or major mental illness (schizophrenia), have spectacular islands of ability or brilliance which stand in stark, markedly incongruous contrast to the handicap.

The ability or brilliance, while spectacular, occurs within a very narrow range considering all the skills in the human repertoire. It occurs generally in one of the following areas: calendar calculating; music, almost exclusively limited to the piano; lightning calculating and mathematics; art, including painting, drawing or sculpting; mechanical ability; prodigious memory (mnemonism); or very rarely, unusual sensory discrimination (smell or touch) or extrasensory perception.

savant (sav'ənt), n., man of learning and science. [<earlier F ppr. of SAVOIR know < L SAPERE be wise]

— Darold A. Treffert, M.D.
Extraordinary People

SCIENCE: In England during the plague of 1665, it was fashionable for doctors to wear robes made of leather which reached the ground. They added gauntlets, broad-brimmed hats and hoods which covered their faces. The hoods had eyepieces made of glass and a bird-like beak which was stuffed with herbs to filter the air. The doctors believed that these clothes would protect them from plague germs. Whether or not this was true, they must have presented a terrifying sight to their patients.

— Wood & Dicks

What They Don't Teach You About History

SENSATIONAL: In 1970 Christine Hubbock ended her life in a sensational and public way. She was an American television newsreader who shot herself in the head in the middle of a programme: 'And now, in keeping with Channel 40's policy of always bringing you the latest in blood and guts, in living colour, you're about to see another first — an attempted suicide.'

— Robert Wilkins, <u>Death</u>

SIGHT: Two centuries ago, William Blake claimed that he did not see with his eyes but looked through them as a pane of glass; we should learn to see creatively, he said, using active rather than passive vision. About thirty years ago the scientific community found that our eyes cannot convey light to our brain. The retina does not "collect light waves" and send them to visual receptors in our brain. Vision is a construction of the brain that we see with the help of our eyes when it refers to this outer world.

— Joseph Chilton Pearce, <u>Evolution's End</u>

SIGNS: I used to wait for a sign, she said, before I did anything. Then one night I had a dream & an angel in black tights came to me & said, You can start any time now & then I asked is this a sign & the angel started laughing & I woke up. Now, I think the whole world is filled with signs, but if there's no laughter, I know they're not for me.

— Brian Andreas
<u>Mostly True</u>

SHAM, n. The professions of politicians, the science of doctors, the Knowledge of reviewers, the religion of sensational preachers, and in a word, the world.

— Ambrose Bierce
The Enlarged Devil's Dictionary

STATUS: Suttee — India, Hindu, the burning of wives on the husband's funeral pyre. Nothing so eloquently testified to the lowly social status of women than an expectation that they should not outlive their husbands. There is considerable speculation about the origin of SUTTEE. Some authorities claim that it emanated from a deliberate tampering with Hindu scriptures. The original version ran: "AROCHANTU JANAYO YONIM AGRE" — "Let the mothers advance to the altar first." By a minor alternation the line becomes: "AROCHANTU JANAYO YONIM AGNETH" — "Let the mothers go into the womb of fire." One anthropologist, Max Müller, dubbed this celebrated change of text "perhaps the most flagrant instance of what can be done by an unscrupulous priesthood."

— Robert Wilkins, _Death_

SUCCESS: Woody Allen — Academy Award-winning writer, producer and director — flunked motion picture production at New York University and the City College of New York. He also failed English at New York University.

— Canfield & Hansen, _Chicken Soup for the Soul_

Tt

technology telephone tongue transatlantic true talk tale

The voice (phone) from afar (tele) >

EARLY TELEPHONE TALK

1876   Alexander Graham Bell to unidentified party,
"Don't call me, I'll call you."

1901   Inventor to colleague, "Did you hear, Hubert
Booth has invented a vacuum cleaner? Says, it
will replace Bissell carpet sweepers. Can't see
it myself. He's built it on a horse-drawn
cart and it needs a petrol-driven pump.
There's a long hose attached, but I ask you,
a horse-drawn cart?"

1902   Mavis to her sister, "Celanese underwear,

you say? My, how modern of you! My George says Celanese silk is another name for Acetate rayon. You know, it's the same stuff they use to varnish aircraft."

1903   Atkin Thompson explains his new device to a reporter, "Yes, it's to prevent choking. Frequency of patients choking on their tongues during surgery? Well, how should I know? One is enough, I would think. Do you want me to explain my device or not? Fine, then refrain from asking impertenant questions. It's very simple really, forceps secure the tongue with a tiny pin, leaving only a minute puncture at the tip. Well, it seems like a small price to pay."

1904   Bill Loman, Sr. gives his son advice, "Not sales,
I tell you, advertising. Get into advertising. Listen to
me, young man. I don't want to hear about that
Ford fellow or William Harley and Arthur Davidson
— they're small potatoes. Forty million! That's
what was spent on advertising this year. Being a
salesman will get you an early grave, that's all."

1906   American undertaker Almon Brown Strowger
talking to his mother (who calls him Brown Sugar),
"That's what I'm trying to tell you, Momma, I'm
losing business hand over fist. Yes, it is possible
when the telephone company constantly misdirects
the calls of those poor souls recently bereaved
Where are they going? (Pause) Oh, you mean the
calls? God only knows. But it's in my hands now.
That's what I've phoned to tell you, I've devised

a telephone switching system controlled
automatically by a dial. No more bedevilled
telephone operators."

1906   Ambrose Bierce to Alexander Graham Bell,
"An invention of the devil which abrogates
some of the advantages of making a
disagreeable person keep his distance."

1909   Anonymous call, "That's right, Congress
has banned the import of opium."

1910   Captain of a transatlantic liner to port authorities in Canada, "Please be advised that I have discovered on board the presence of the notorious wife-killer, Dr. Hawley Harvey Crippen, and his mistress Ethel LeNeve. Alert constabulary."

1916   U.S. public health physician, Joseph Goldberger to the warden of a Louisiana penitentiary, "Of course, overcrowding will exacerbate the problem. Yes, I agree, 907 men under one roof is a health risk. But pellagra is not infectious. That's true, left untreated the disease leads to insanity. Sir, they do not need medicine, they need milk. Pellagra is due to a bad diet."

1924   One medical doctor to another, "Yes, yes, of course, amputation of the breasts has been carried out from earliest times, but this is different. Now, with this new Lexer-Kraske operation we can reduce pendulous breasts. Why? My dear doctor, why not? After all, besides improving the appearance of the patient, the operation relieves infertility."

Punki whistles as he wipes down the counter.

"What's that tune?" I ask.

"You don't know?"

"No."

"Where have you been?" Punki sings, "Row, row, row your boat, / Gently down the stream. / Merrily, merrily, merrily, merrily, / Life is but a dream."

Uu

The UFO is the mid-twentieth century's angel.

Mortals are immortals and immortals are mortal —
one lives the other's death and dies the other's life.
                              — Heraclitus

Punki of Punki's CyberCafe called me ubiquitous
the other day. UBIQUITOUS: being everywhere at
the same time; present everywhere. I don't think he
meant it literally. It was more in response to my
inquiring mind and all the things I'm into. (I had
just dropped on him my idea of becoming a
cyberspace undertaker.) It is possible though, that
unconsciously Punki recognizes me. I have never been
able to mask myself against the human unconscious.
Yet, I'm rarely recognized for who I am.

Vv

virtue vice vacation venomous value vile vindicate

ON VIRTUE & BECOMING HUMAN

1. You should know that owls, after repaying their former debts, are reborn as wayward men in the realm of human beings.

2. Inauspicious creatures, after repaying their former debts, are reborn as men with animal habits.

3. Foxes, after repaying their former debts, are reborn as vulgar men.

4. Venomous creatures, after repaying their former debts, are reborn as savages.

5. Tapeworms, after repaying their former debts, are reborn as vile men.

6. Creatures good for food, after repaying their former debts, are reborn as cowards.

7. Animals providing material for wearing apparel, after repaying their former debts, are reborn as servile men.

8. Creatures through whom the future can be foretold, after repaying their former debts, are reborn as literary men.

9. Auspicious creatures, after repaying their former debts, are reborn as intelligent men.

10. Domestic animals, after repaying their former debts, are reborn as men versed in the ways of the world.

Ānanda, these living beings, after repaying their debts, are reborn in the realm of human beings because since the time without beginning, they have, on account of their Karma and perversion, killed one another and have not met the Buddha or heard the right Dharma, hence their transmigration according to the law of samāra; they are most pitiable.
(China, 8th Century A.D.)

— David Meltzer
<u>Death: An Anthology of Ancient Texts,</u>
<u>Songs, Prayers and Stories.</u>

Ww

They've tacked her crayon drawings to the walls of the cafe. Someone asks her mom why she draws wax fruit and vegetables. Why not the real thing? The interlocuter thinks the artist cannot speak for herself. She is eight years old.

"Real fruit's for eating," is what her mom says as she stiffens the foam on a cappuccino.

Wax crayons, wax fruit, wax vegetables: art imitating artifice = life. The life of this child line by minute by stroke; her mind absorbed in red, green, yellow, orange. The mind absorbed in making — the great human escape.

The making of wax wings is one thing, flying too close to the sun is another. Daedalus' son Icarus plummeted to earth when his wings melted. Is that what happens

when the young artist must put
her crayons back in their orange
box? Does she plummet to earth? Is that
why she can turn her back on the fruits of her
labour, leave them on walls buffeted by the
air conditioning and walk away with her hand
in her mom's?

Outside they walk past the doors of the
Glenbow Museum; I turn and go in. I have a
job with security here. This includes a grey and
blue uniform and a walkie talkie. I keep people
from touching the objects of their curiosity, their
appreciation, their desire. Museums are of
and for the eye. The body is a liability. The
exhibition floors are quiet in the way
churches and sacred caves are. That's why
I work here; I like quiet.

The exhibitions are a constant source of surprise — human escape takes many forms. A magic act. I stand at the door to Aganetha Dyck's <u>Extended Wedding Party</u> and watch honeybees make a strapless gown. Inside a plexiglass case is a glass dress-form honeycombed with a rich lace of wax. The bees come and go through a clear plastic tunnel extended between the case and a hole in the roof. The bride is in the process of becoming, while the rest of the wedding party waits nearby — robes, suits, hats, shoes in rich, deep colours layered with paint and wax into stiff, bodiless garments. These clothes-in-waiting hang in metal closets made from used Queen bee

excluders (screens rusty with wax). The shoes
are bee fantasies.

The audacity of the woman, this Aganetha
Dyck, to form an artistic partnership with
insects. And to allow the insects to remake
the objects of ordinary human existence.
Besides hats, shoes, dresses there are bee sculpted
figurines and crystal bowls; encased in honey-
brown wax are women's purses, briefcases,
books, phonograph records.

Standing at the door of the exhibition
hall, I flip through the museum's guidebook
to Aganetha Dyck.

Born late in the Depression and raised on a Manitoba farm near Marquette by her immigrant Mennonite parents, Dyck's sense of beauty is intimately connected to a sense of the well-worn, the used, the second-hand, to objects that make up the fabric of daily existence.

"The ritual of the wedding and the cult of the bride are as fascinating as the reproductive rituals of the honey bees and their queen," says Aganetha Dyck. The Extended Wedding Party consists of a glass wedding dress which is in its third season of production along with various attendants, garments sewn out of hive blankets and suspended between hive screens. Included in the installation is food for the wedding feast, various wedding gifts and a multitude of shoes. Together they present a silent, haunting image of decay and development. By emphasizing the absence of the human body Dyck speaks to what is missing.

I enter.

There is no hot light here, mindful of Icarus. To walk into this room is to enter hive twilight redolent with the clean warmth of honeycomb. I wish I could bring the girl artist from the cafe here. What would she make of this world? Would she want to draw and colour what is no longer strictly manmade? Her drawings improve on the factory-made wax fruit, because her free hand cannot produce a perfect circle, oval, straightline. Could she improve on what the bees have done? Would she want to? I think she would find a corner, lay out her scrapbook on the floor, take out her box of Crayolas and make something of her own.

But she is the exception. Most of the people who walk through this room are awestruck and confused. The bees go about their business.

"They say the proud are reborn as bees."
                    – Martin Buber, Ten Rungs: Hasidic Sayings

"The parameters of the bumblebee's universe may be determined by the wave-frequency of purple, not time-space dimensions as in ours."
                    – Joseph Chilton Pearce, Evolution's End

Xx

Xmas xylophone xenophobia xerography X-ray xebec xanthous Xeroxes

THE STORY OF X

The 14th letter of the Greek alphabet; the 24th letter of this alphabet; the Roman numeral for 10; a term to designate a person, thing, agency, factor, or the like whose true name is unknown or withheld; an unknown quantity.

Thorndike · Barnhart Dictionary

Xx/eks/n. (as x) first unknown quantity in algebra; cross-shaped symbol esp. used to indicate position (X marks the spot) or incorrectness or to symbolize a kiss or vote, or as signature of person who cannot write.

The Oxford Dictionary of Current English

X in our alphabet being a needless letter has added invincibility to the attacks of the spelling reformers, and like them, will doubtless last as long as the language. X is the sacred symbol of ten dollars, and in such words as Xmax, Xn, etc., stands for Christ, not as is popularly supposed, because it represents a cross, but because the corresponding letter in the Greek alphabet is the initial of his name.... If it represented a cross it would stand for St. Andrew, who "testified" upon one of that shape. In the algebra of psychology x stands for Woman's mind.

—Ambrose Bierce
<u>The Enlarged Devil's Dictionary</u>

X the unknown, the unknowable.

X the mysterious, as arcane as a kiss, as unpredictable as a vote.

X the paradox, that definitive spot on a treasure map, the ten of any Roman numeral sequence found at the end of movies (not on the screen long enough to be deciphered by Arabic trained minds).

Ambrose Bierce thought it a needless letter; I think it's an essential letter: Every system must contain at least one paradox. A system as powerful as language must always be reminded of its inherent contradictions.

As for the claim that x is the symbol of "Woman's mind," I have to wonder what letter represents "Man's mind"? Nothing, I hazard, as complex and intriguing as X.

It's surprising that X hasn't caught on in advertising. It's open to many more possibilities than the other letters of the alphabet already in use:

K=car K=potassium K=kilo K=carat K=king K= 1000 word

Xerox, as a company, connected itself with the process of xerography, but in going from the Greek _xeros_ (dry) to Xerox they boldly went beyond dry by adding another x. To begin and end yourself with an X is to acknowledge the paradoxical nature of human endeavour.

Yy

yore yes you yearn yield yellow

We're at the Mountain Equipment Co-op. I'm buying my first tent and have asked a friend to advise me. She is immensely qualified: a doctor of archaeology (think of the field trips), a first-rate mountain climber and seasoned expedition organizer with peaks on five continents to her credit. I've been invited to join her and Sharon Wood for a climbing weekend in the Rockies around Banff.

When I arrived at the Mountain Equipment Co-op, late, I found my friend, Hela, sitting on the steps reading The National Enquirer.

"You," I accuse, "Dr. Sigurd, reading a tabloid! The yellow press!"

She doesn't look up. "You never know what you'll learn..."

"Learn?"

"About what we fear." Hela holds up the paper. "Look, monsters of all sizes and shapes."

"I want your expert opinion. Is this or is this not sensational trash?"

"My grandmother used to tell me the old stories about the Norse Gods and my Mom would complain that Nan was giving me nightmares. And she did. It took all my courage to fall asleep in the dark. But if I showed my fear, there would be no more stories — Mom would see to that. I'd say Nan's stories were sensational."

"It's not the same," I say, scandalized. "That's tradition, folklore, mythology."

"I didn't care how old the stories were, they were scary stories and I loved to hear them. Gods and giants,

heroes and gnomes. But my greatest
fear was always for Yggdrasil, a
wonderous ash tree, whose roots and
branches bound together heaven and
earth and hell."

"No goddesses in these stories?"

"Only one, my namesake, Hela."

"Of course."

"Hela rules the Kingdom of Death. To
quote my grandmother, 'No god had any
authority there, not Odin, even. Asgard the Golden
belonged to the gods; glorious Valhalla to the heroes;
Midgard was the battlefield for men, not the business
of women. Gudrun, in the Elder Edda says, THE
FIERCENESS OF MEN RULES THE FATE OF WOMEN.
The cold pale world of the shadowy dead was
woman's sphere in Norse mythology.'"

"So, you pinned your hopes on a tree?"

"Vain, though they were. You see, in Norse tradition everything including the gods are doomed and all ends in death. A serpent and his brood gnaw continually at the roots of Yggdrasil. They will succeed in killing the tree someday and the universe will come crashing down."

"I can see why you were drawn to archaeology."

"One for you," Hela laughs.

"What you're reading in the tabs, then, is modern mythology?"

"Two for you." She folds the paper and stands. "What was it we came here for?"

"A tent."

"Ah, yes, a miniature, nylon universe. What colour will you buy?"

"Colour? What does that matter?"

"It matters, believe me, try seven solid days trapped in a snowstorm on Annapurna."

"I doubt I'll ever have to worry about snowstorms in the Himalayas."

"We could get weathered-in on Mount Temple."

"That's where your taking me!"

"How do you feel about yellow? Depending on who you listen to, it will either make you feel warm, golden and blessed, or you will envy your companions' stories and try to undermine them. Red will make you angry. Blue will give you hallucinations about flying. Orange will make you reckless."

"Are you planning to tell me more of your grandmother's stories?"

"No. I'll lend you her book. You can read them for yourself. She was Edith Hamilton, the classicist."

"Yellow should do fine."

Zz

zeal zenith zeitgeist zero zoo

Z IS FOR GYPSY

I started eating words when I was a child. The first I tasted were ARBEIT MACHT FREI. At the time everything was food for thought, bad tasting and good. Then I had ZUGANG shoved down my throat, upon arriving, before the distraction of numbers. I choked; they laughed. I spit out their words; they laughed harder. I had not been showered, not been registered. They ran their fingers through my hair. It would be stored, EFFEKTENKAMMER. I'd get it back, they said, when I left the camp. I went on to eat numbers. Long after I stopped fingering the scar on the inside of my arm. It was much later and only came about because eating words in my new life limited me to birthday cake. I got into numbers by accident. They came on a baby Gouda from Safeway, Dutch numbers, close enough. The more I ate, the more completely the numbers on my arm faded. Now, in order to read my scar, I must do it with my fingertips, like Braille. Except for the 2. What I know is... I disgorged all the words I ever swallowed, blotting them up with paper. I see again the sign over the main entrance to Auschwitz #1, WORK WILL SET YOU FREE. The barracks for newcomers who still thought of themselves as free. The storehouse where I worked sorting hair by colour.

DEATH NOTICES

DIGITAL IMMORTALITY — A SLICE

THE INTERNET has immortalized the body of an unknown woman donated to science.

"Called the Visible Woman, she joins the Visible Man as billions of digital bits that together constitute the most detailed images of the human body ever assembled."

The digital bits are obtained by freezing the cadavers, depositing them in gelatin and then slicing them into very thin sections." These fine pieces of human anatomy were photographed digitally creating high resolution images.

"The male body was cut into slices one centimeter thick. Aided by that experience, researchers were able to slice the woman into slices only one-third as thick, making the images derived far more detailed."

"The thought of suicide is a great consolation: by means of it one gets successfully through many a bad night."

— Nietzche, who else!

Our Swedish birthday boy Kurt Jarlson plunged from his seventh floor flat dressed as the Grim Reaper. Mr. Jarlson, of Stockholm had dreamt every night for 30 years that he'd die before he was 50. So overjoyed was he to be alive on the morning of his 50th birthday that he arranged a massive jamboree to toast his survival. 'Kurt was dressed as Death, with a big scythe,' explained one party goer. 'He was running around shouting "I'm alive—" but then he fell out the window.' The story doesn't end there, however, for as Mr. Jarlson tumbled earthwards he was spotted by 85-year-old Ingar Gunterrson, who cried 'Just one more year, Father Death!' before promptly suffering a terminal coronary.

Two, in one blow

Love, death and odd ends

Last summer, a man in Sao Paulo, Brazil, caught his wife in bed with her lover, and glued her hands to the man's penis. Doctors separated the two, but the man died from toxic chemicals absorbed through the skin.

A 22-year-old Peruvian woman died of septicemic poisoning in June after the rusty padlock on the leather chastity belt that her jealous husband forced her to wear dug into her flesh and caused an infection.

Ménage à deux et demie

When the Perón regime in Argentina fell to a coup in 1955, Juan Perón went to live in Madrid, Spain. From there, Perón orchestrated the kidnapping of his dead wife, Evita Perón. Because she was so loved by the people of Argentina, the new government of President Colonel Pedro Avamburu planned to dispose of Evita Perón's body and therefore remove an important symbol for the Peronist movement.

Juan Perón succeeded in bringing his wife's body to Spain where "she was installed in a new room of the second floor of Perón's Madrid home. He was now living with his third wife, but this detail seems not to have interfered with an easy transition into a ménage à trois, or perhaps more appropriately, à deux et demie. The evening meal was taken by the married couple in the same room where Evita reposed."

'To be or not to be,' the ultimate in self inflicted death.

An old and persistent theory has it that every ejaculation of semen takes a day off a man's life . . . .

HEART BURN

In 1822, the English poet, Percy Shelley, drowned in the Mediterranean. His friends, Edward Trelawny and Lord Byron, were forbidden to bury him. "When his body was washed ashore, the Tuscan quarantine laws, drafted to protect against imported plague, laid down that the body was to be burned on the beach. . . . Shelley's ashes were buried in the Protestant cemetery in Rome, but the poet's heart, which had failed to burn, was plucked from the flames by Trelawny and subsequently returned to Britain for burial."

Critics are born killers. Albert Camus made sure this anecdote made it into his book, The Myth of Sisyphus.

I have heard of a post-war writer who, after having finished his first book, committed suicide to attract attention to his work. Attention was in fact attracted, but the book was judged no good.

Early nineteenth-century French novelist Eugène Sue's mistress may have found the ultimate in body recycling. At her explicit request, a set of his books was bound in skin taken from her corpse's shoulders. These books were sold by Foyles bookshop in London in 1951 for $29.

Shortly after the Jacobite Rebellions (1715-1745) a man was sentenced to death and hanged in York for playing his bagpipes. Bagpipes had been classified as an instrument of war and outlawed. (Heard this on the radio)

The bloodiest civil war in history was fought in China. The peasant rebels were led by Hong Xuiquan, who believed he was the younger brother of Jesus Christ. Hong called the war T'ai P'ing , which means 'Great Peace.' During the war, which lasted from 1851-1864, roughly 30 million people died. Faced with final defeat Hong . . . killed himself by eating gold leaf — surely one of the most exotic and expensive methods of committing suicide ever devised!

Mad men have such an appetite for destruction. Is this true of mad women?

KING **SENNACHERIB** OF Ancient Assyria hated careless parking. He decreed that the penalty for wrongly parking a chariot or cart in his capital city of Nimeveh should be death by impalement.

High Stakes!

FUN ON THE SLAB

Tales of sex and death, which historically have had male sexism as their hallmark, may have recently taken something of a turn toward sympathetic treatment of women. If this is so, it is an example of shifting social norms and standards of popular culture influencing a hardy breed of joke: the cadaver story. . . . 'In a variation on another traditional story line, the female victim (a medical student) does not faint with shock when she discovers a penis stuck in her cadaver's vagina. Instead she masterfully escapes the intended victim status by turning to the expectant male audience with a cavalier, *I see one of you pulled out too quickly last night.*'

Screaming like a banshee, bargaining like a waterfront drug dealer, bleeding like a side of beef in an abattoir, the Chinese sailor croaked out one word: 'Firelight' (a code word? or a dying man's resurrection of a beloved childhood memory?) and fell to the ground, sprawled out like an electrocuted lobster, clutching in his fist loosened by the merciful kiss of death fire of another sort: a 20-carat, flawless blue diamond.

— The epitome of death scenes. Citizen Kane pales by comparison.

"The mental anguish of being selected a human sacrifice, tied to the altar and about to go to glory, was enough to send the young twenty-year-old warrior's blood pressure sky-high."

From the Slush Pile, excerpts culled from unsolicited manuscripts sent to a prominent editor of serious fiction.

"I am dying beyond my means."
Oscar Wilde,
impoverished writer

THE WORD 'THUG' comes from a Hindi word describing the followers of the cult of thuggee. The thugs were required by their religion to murder and then rob their victims in honor of Kali, the Hindu goddess of destruction. They were not allowed to spill blood so their method of killing was to strangle their victims with a silk scarf weighted at one end with a coin. It is estimated that over 2,000,000 Indians were strangled by thugs between the years 1550 and 1853.

KALI MADE ME DO IT!

"A MOTHER WHO DISAPPROVED of her daughter's fiancé killed herself at the wedding reception. A California woman lay across the tracks in front of the commuter train on which she knew her husband was returning home. One July 4, a thirty-year-old New York man, depressed over breaking up with his girlfriend, stuck a powerful firecracker in his mouth, lit it, and blew himself up on the front steps of her home."

Madness in the method

"I pray you, see me up safe — and for my coming down, let me shift for myself."

— Sir Thomas More, speaking to the hangman at his execution in 1535

Marching to a different drummer

One man supposedly asked Harvard's Anatomical Museum to cover two drumheads with his skin. One was to be inscribed with the Pope's 'Universal Prayer,' and the other with the 'Declaration of Independence.' A friend was instructed to beat the rhythm of *Yankee Doodle* at the foot of Bunker Hill each July 17 on these skin-covered drums. No one knows if the friend complied with this bizarre request.

Slip of a tongue, death of a nation — human irony

IN BJÖRN KURTÉN'S *Dance of the Tiger* the Neanderthals' speech is incomplete, because they can't make the vowel sounds *aw*, *ee* and *oo* (as in hot, heat and hoot). This seemingly slight impediment is the basis for one scientific explanation of why the Neanderthals died out. . . . Lieberman and Crelin have never argued that the lack of these sounds meant that the Neanderthals couldn't speak, but it would, they think, have made their speech slightly less intelligible, slightly more prone to error, and slower. If they were in competition for the somewhat scanty resources of Ice Age Europe with people who had modern larynxes and so could make the entire range of modern speech sounds, that slightly poorer speech might have been their undoing.

YOU LIGHT UP MY LIFE!

A Frenchman who had been betrayed by his mistress planned his suicide in minute detail. Before killing himself he called his servant and gave orders that after death a candle should be made from his fat and carried, lighted, to his mistress. To accompany it he wrote a note saying that, just as he had burned for her in life, so would he after his death. Proof of his passion she would find in the light by which she read his letter — a flame fed by his miserable body!

The red stripe on a barber's pole symbolizes blood.

DID YOU KNOW that many people believe that having a haircut reduces a person's physical strength, just like the story of Samson? Fijiian chiefs, for instance, were so fearful of being weakened by the barber that they used to eat a man before having a haircut!

Sardaine is a type of root whose effects were described by an Italian author in 1544: 'Those who die from having eaten it look like a person laughing.' The sardonic laugh is the laugh of the skeleton.

"Grimace," a more expressive word.

I am a woman, 82 years old and I just posed nude for a photographer. He is called a documentary photographer and I am the naked document. He has a theory, I have eternal sleep. I wasn't seduced by his ideas of a counter - imagery of the grotesque, visual rhetoric, multiple versions of decisive moments, even though he wrote them in a letter. It was a chance to see myself, get outside the skin, like dying and being revived.

← STILL LIFE AND NUDE

Where do you suppose they hung these paintings: parlour, dining room, kitchen, bedroom, guest room?

The skeleton, as a principle figure in the imagined world of death, "was born from the development of anatomy in the sixteenth and seventeenth centuries. Science in those days was not limited to a small elite. . . . People would have their pictures painted grouped around a dissection table, just as they would around a banquet or card table or at a musical concert. Science, death, and a kind of fascination combined to inspire a coherent iconography not unlike the comic strips of today.

The surrealist poet Robert Desnos is being taken away from the barracks of the concentration camp where he has been held prisoner. Leaving the barracks, the mood is somber; everyone knows the truck is headed for the gas chambers. And when the truck arrives no one can speak at all; even the guards fall silent. But this silence is soon interrupted by an energetic man [Desnos], who jumps into the line and grabs one of the condemned. Desnos reads the man's palm. *Oh ,* he says, *I see you have a very long lifeline. And you are going to have three children.* And his excitement is contagious. First one man, then another, offers up his hand, and the prediction is for longevity, more children, abundant joy.

As Desnos reads more palms, not only does the mood of the prisoners change but that of the guards too. How can one explain it? Perhaps the element of surprise has planted a shadow of doubt in their minds. If they told themselves these deaths were inevitable, this no longer seems inarguable. They are in any case so disoriented by this sudden change of mood among those they are about to kill that they are unable to go through with the executions. So all the men, along with Desnos, are packed back into the truck and taken back to the barracks. Desnos has saved his own life and the lives of others by using his imagination.

IMAGINE THAT

May you be in heaven an hour before the devil knows you're dead.

Old Irish Blessing

SIGNS OF DEATH IN NEWFOUNDLAND:

Three lamps lighted together mean death.

An old, disused clock strikes and signifies death.

If a blind falls down, some one in the house will soon die.

Rapping on the side of house means death.

If a girl is married in black, one of the couple will die.

Leaving part of a potato bed unplanted means death within the year.

A hollow square, coffin-shaped, in a boiled pudding signifies death.

On the death of a first child in a family, all its clothes must be given away, or the succeeding children will die.

It's unlucky to put the baby to a looking-glass before he's a year old. The child will die.

Several cadavers have remained incorrupt for over 700 years. St. Sperandia, who died in 1270, was last examined by a scientific team in 1952. Her skin was dry but still naturally coloured; her body generally was 'intact, flexible, and exhaling a suave fragrance.'

There are 102 bodies documented as incorruptible. Some 36 or more are on public display. Apparently these bodies have never been embalmed.

Death without decay is still death, never to be confused with sleep. St. Bernadette only looks like she is sleeping in her glass case in Nevers, France. Saints preserve.

The birth of death. To contend and negotiate with the invisible. To order, to divide and separate, day from night, spirit from flesh. By inventing death man creates his desire for immortality. It's the beginning of language and the beginning of philosophy. Death's invention is the beginning of time and the end of nature. Man is the center of what surrounds him, the center of the cosmos.

The invention of death, its entry into symbol, language, into the creating imagination, is the beginning of myth and ritual.

Fear and awe, an awareness of our humanity. The corpse could just as well be me. I live surrounded by death who has my face in his pocket.

David Meltzer

> **"I feel the daisies growing over me."**
> John Keats, poet.

> **"Now comes the mystery."**
> Henry Ward Beecher, 19th century American orator

A truly memorable memorial is Sir Richard (Francis) Burton's tent in the Catholic churchyard of St. Mary Magdalen at Mortlake, south London. Burton (1821–90) was the archetypal Victorian adventurer: heavily disguised, he was the first white man to enter Mecca; in the Crimean War he commanded the Turkish cavalry; in 1856, with John Speke, he was unsuccessful in his attempt to discover the source of the Nile. When he died, in 1890, his wife, Lady Isobel . . . applied to have him join Speke and Livingstone in Westminster Abbey. Permission was refused, probably because of Burton's translations of books about the sexual habits of primitives, including *The Perfumed Garden* and *Kama Sutra*. St. Paul's Cathedral was no more forgiving. Eventually it was proposed to build an enormous stone tent in order to honour this remarkable man.

Richard and Isobel, the original happy campers.

ROBERT LIVINGSTONE'S heart (as in 'Mr. Livingstone, I presume') was buried in Africa after he died; his body was returned to Westminster Abbey. Although Frédéric Chopin's heart is in the church of the Holy Cross in Warsaw, his body is at Père-Lachaise, Paris, France. (His French tomb is often used as a mailbox for lovers.) Likewise, when noted physicist Albert Einstein died in 1955, most of his body was cremated and his ashes scattered. His brain, however, was preserved by a Princeton Hospital pathologist for analysis, since Einstein's was purportedly the most brilliant mind of the twentieth century. (At two and two-thirds pounds, it was hardly of extraordinary size, as the average weight of a male human's brain is three pounds.)

Size is not at the heart of the matter

Beheading, an 'easy' death if carried out with skill, was reserved exclusively for condemned nobles or people of importance . . . plebians were executed — and we are speaking now only of those executions that did not intentionally prescribe painful methods — in ways that caused prolonged agonies. . . . As we have noted in the case of The Guillotine, a head cut off with a swift and neat slash is fully aware of its fate as it rolls along the ground or falls into the basket. Perception is extinguished only after a few seconds.

"I think, therefore, I am."

Since the death rate is relatively constant, funeral homes often ruthlessly compete with each other for business. In the United States, funeral homes (and cemeteries) rely on obnoxious telephone and direct mail advertising. This is mild, however, compared to Thailand where two 'charity' burial organizations, the *Por Teck Tueng* and *Ruamkatany* monitor police radios and use lights and sirens to speed to accident scenes to retrieve bodies, often arriving before the police. Not infrequently, their representatives fight over the right to collect a body. Each group claims that the other does this to extort money from the victims' relatives.

Funeral home!
Funeral home: a contradiction
of terms. I much
prefer the
ancient Egyptians'
House of Vigor.

Groped up, to see if God was there —
Groped backward at Himself
Caressed a Trigger absently
And wandered out of Life.

(The enigmatic Emily) Dickinson,
'He scanned it'

Corpses are embalmed for two main reasons: public health and public viewing. Public health reasons are, at best, questionable; public viewing is an American cultural phenomenon.

Early Christians rejected embalming as a pagan practice that mutilated the corpse, although some exceptions were made for exalted persons, such as Charlemagne who died and was embalmed in A.D. 814. It was not until the time of the American Civil War that modern embalming, again for religious or at least sentimental purposes, took hold.

Embalmers, also called: throat cutters, belly punchers, barber-surgeons and monks.

"I feel as if I were to be myself again."
Sir Walter Scott, novelist and poet

"All my possessions for a moment of time."
Queen Elizabeth I

"I imagined it was more difficult to die."
Louis XIV of France

I am amazed that so many people are troubled by her, since she is within us every second and should be accepted with resignation. How should one have such great fear of a person with whom one cohabits, who is closely mingled with our own substance? But there it is. One has grown used to making a fable of her and to judging her from outside. Better to tell oneself that at birth one marries her and to make the best of her disposition, however deceitful it may be. For she knows how to make herself forgotten and to let us believe that she no longer inhabits the house. Each one of us houses his own death and reassures himself by what he invents about her — namely that she is an allegorical figure only appearing in the last act.

Jean Cocteau

"I was born without knowing why, I have lived without knowing why, and I am dying without either knowing why or how."

Pierre Gassendi, French philosopher

Death Sources

Sources listed for clippings by page from top to bottom:

Abrams, M.H., et al. *The Norton Anthology of English Literature*. 3rd ed. Vol. 1. New York: W.W. Norton, 1974.

Allen, R.E. *Oxford Dictionary of Current English*. Oxford: Oxford University Press, 1985.

Andreas, Brian. *Mostly True*. Decorah, IA: StoryPeople, 1993.

Ariès, Phillippe. *The Hour of Our Death*. Trans. Helen Weaver. New York: Alfred A. Knopf, 1981.

---. *Images of Man and Death*. Trans. Janet Lloyd. Cambridge: Harvard University Press, 1985.

---. *Western Attitudes Toward Death from the Middle Ages to the Present*. Trans. Patricia M. Ranum. Baltimore: The John Hopkins University Press, 1974.

Barnhart, Clarence L. *Thorndike • Barnhart Dictionary*. New York: Doubleday, 1967.

Beckett, Samuel. *Endgame: A Play in One Act*. New York: Grove Press, 1958.

Berger, Arthur, et al. *Perspectives on Death and Dying*. Philadelphia: The Charles Press, 1989.

Berger, John. *Ways of Seeing*. London: Penguin Books, 1972.

Biedermann, Hans. *Dictionary of Symbolism*. Trans. James Hulbert. New York: Penguin Books, 1992.

Bierce, Ambrose. *The Enlarged Devil's Dictionary*. Ed. Ernest J. Hopkins. New York: Doubleday, 1967.

Blanch, Lesley. *The Wilder Shores of Love*. London: Orion Books, 1993.

Bowen, Gail. *A Killing Spring*. Toronto: McClelland & Stewart, 1996.

Canfield, Jack, and Mark Victor Hansen. *A 2nd Helping of Chicken Soup for the Soul*. Deerfield Beach, FL: Health Communications, 1995.

"Can Imagination Save Us?" *Utne Reader* July-Aug. 1996: n. pag.

Chadwick, John C. *Folklore and Witchcraft in Dorset and Wiltshire*. Lyme Regis, UK: N.J. Clarke Publications, n.d.

Chadwick, Nora. *The Celts*. London: Penguin Books, 1971.

Colombo, John Robert. *The Dictionary of Canadian Quotations*. Toronto: Stoddart, 1991.

Costello, Matthew J. *The Greatest Games of All Times*. New York: John Wiley & Sons, 1991.

Crystal, David, ed. *The Cambridge Encyclopedia*. Cambridge: Cambridge University Press, 1990.

de Laszlo, Violet S., ed. *The Basic Writings of C. G. Jung*. New York: Random House, 1959.

Duncan, Doree, et al. *Life Into Art, Isadora Duncan and her World*. New York: W.W. Norton, 1993.

Duryer, Maggie. ed. *Aganetha Dyck*. Winnipeg: Winnipeg Art Gallery, 1995.

Enright, D. J., ed. *The Oxford Book of Death*. Oxford: Oxford University Press, 1987.

Estés, Clarissa Pinkola. *The Radiant Coat*. Audiocassette. N.p: n.p., n.d.

Feldman, Fred. *Confrontations With the Reaper: A Philosophical Study of the Nature and Value of Death*. New York: Oxford University Press, 1994.

Ford, John. *Tutankhamen's Treasures*. Don Mills, ON: Thomas Nelson & Sons, 1978.

"From the Slush Pile." *National Lampoon* Feb. 1984: n. pag.

Garrison, Webb. *Strange Facts About Death.* Nashville: Parthenon Press, 1978.

Gonzalez-Crussi, F. *The Day of the Dead and Other Mortal Reflections.* New York: Harcourt-Brace, 1993.

Hamilton, Edith. *Mythology: Timeless Tales of Gods and Heroes.* Boston: Little, Brown, 1942.

Harpur, Patrick, ed. *The Timetable of Technology.* New York: Hearst Books, 1982.

Head To Toe: Personal Adornment Around the World. Calgary: Glenbow-Alberta Institute, 1994.

Hoban, Fairfield W. *The Pleasures of Learning Chess.* Toronto: Van Nostrand Reinhold, 1982.

"How Dangerous One's Birthday Can Be." *Spare Change* 15 Jan. 1996: n. pag.

"The Incorruptibles." *Alberta Report* 3 June 1996: n. pag.

Ingram, Jay. *Talk Talk Talk: An Investigation Into the Mystery of Speech.* Toronto: Penguin Books, 1992.

Inquisitor: Modus Informata Extrahere 1.3 (1994).

Iserson, Kenneth V. *Death to Dust.* Tucson, AZ: Galen Press, 1994.

Janson, H. W. *History of Art.* New York: Harry N. Abrams, 1973.

King, Laurie R. *The Beekeeper's Apprentice.* New York: Bantam Books, 1996.

Kroetsch, Robert. Epigram. *Prairie Fire* 17.2 (1996): n. pag.

Lederer, Richard. *The Play of Words.* New York: Simon & Schuster, 1990.

Macrone, Michael. *Eureka! What Archimedes Really Meant.* New York: Cader Books, 1994.

Meltzer, David, ed. *Death: An Anthology of Ancient Texts, Songs, Prayers, and Stories.* San Francisco: North Point Press, 1984.

Michaels, Anne. *Fugitive Pieces.* Toronto: McClelland & Stewart, 1996.

Morse, Kitty. *Edible Flowers.* N.p.: Ten Speed Press, 1995.

Nikiforuk, Andrew. *The Fourth Horseman: A Short History of Epidemics, Plagues, Famine and Other Scourges.* Toronto: Penguin Books, 1991.

Nuland, Sherwin B. *How We Die.* New York: Random House, 1993.

O'Farrell, Padraic. *Before The Devil Knows You're Dead.* Dublin: Mercier Press, 1993.

Ondaatje, Michael. *The Collected Works of Billy the Kid.* Toronto: Anansi, 1970.

Orenstein, Larry. "Stabbed to Death With a Cheese One Way to Go for the Odd Enders." *Globe & Mail* n.d.: n. pag.

Partridge, Eric. *Origins: A Short Etymological Dictionary of Modern English.* New York: Greenwich House, 1983.

Pearce, Joseph Chilton. *Evolution's End: Claiming the Potential of Our Intelligence.* San Francisco: HarperCollins, 1992.

"Perón's Body To Be Dug Up." *Daily Express* 31 Aug. 1996: n. pag.

"Pictogram Designer Paul Arthur Gives Orders to the Planet – Without Using A Single Word." *Equinox* Oct. 1994: n. pag.

"Quit Pro Quotes." *Utne Reader* Sept.-Oct. 1996: n. pag.

Rheingold, Howard. *Virtual Reality*. New York: Summit Books, 1991.

Rice, Scott. *It Was a Dark and Stormy Night*. New York: Penguin Books, 1984.

Salmonson, Jessica A. *The Encyclopedia of Amazons*. New York: Paragon House, 1991.

Saul, John Ralston. *The Doubter's Companion*. Toronto: Penguin Books, 1994.

"Scientists Offer 'The End Of Death.'" *Calgary Herald* 18 July 1996: n. pag.

Stevens, Serita D., and Anne Klarner. *Deadly Doses: A Writer's Guide to Poisons*. Cincinnati: Writer's Digest Books, 1990.

"Still Life & Nude." *Border Crossings* 13.2 (1994): n. pag.

Taber, Clarence W. *Taber's Cyclopedic Medical Dictionary*. Toronto: Ryerson Press, 1970.

Thorson, James A. "Did You Ever See A Hearse Go By? Some Thoughts on Gallows Humour." *Journal of American Culture* 16.2 (1993): n. pag.

Toufexis, Anastasia. "Monster Mice: Scientists Breed Ferocious Rodents That Rape and Kill." *Time Magazine* n.d.: n. pag.

Treffert, Donald A. *Extraordinary People: Understanding Savant Syndrome*. New York: Ballantine Books, 1989.

Tripp, Rhoda Thomas. *The International Thesaurus of Quotations*. New York: Harper & Row, 1970.

Trippett, Frank. *The First Horsemen*. New York: Time-Life Books, 1974.

"'Virtual Woman'" Lives On In Cyberspace." *Calgary Herald* 30 Nov. 1995: n. pag.

Weir, Robert, ed. *Death in Literature*. New York: Columbia University Press, 1980.

Wilkins, Robert. *Death: A History of Man's Obsessions & Fears*. New York: Barnes & Noble, 1990.

Wood, Tim, and Ian Dicks. *What They Don't Teach You About History*. New York: Derrydale Books, 1990.

Darlene Barry Quaife is on the bookshelves of your bookstore/cafe. Look for her novels *Bone Bird* and *Days & Nights on the Amazon*. While you're there, check out who's drinking coffee and writing at the table near the window.